Explore the World of
Mighty Oceans

Text by Susan Wells

Illustrated by Sebastian Quigley

A GOLDEN BOOK • NEW YORK

Western Publishing Company, Inc., Racine, Wisconsin 53404

Contents

What does the ocean floor look like?
Beneath the surface of the oceans there are
dramatic ridges, like mountain ranges, with vast, flat
plains and rolling hills on either side. Some of the
ridges rise above the surface of the water to form
islands. Much of the ocean floor is about 2 miles
deep, but in some places there are trenches about
7 miles deep.

What is a warm-water vent?

In some parts of the oceans, particularly in the Pacific Ocean, there are vents, or cracks, in the ocean floor through which hot water blows. These often look like chimneys and are called "smokers," because the water is full of sulfur and looks like smoke. The hot water and sulfur come from the fiery, molten interior of the Earth and warm the surrounding water. Although very few animals can live in the cold, dark waters of the deep ocean, some unusual ones live in the warm waters surrounding the vents. Strange tube worms, limpets, clams, snails, sea anemones, crabs, and even some fish are found there.

More about warm-water vents

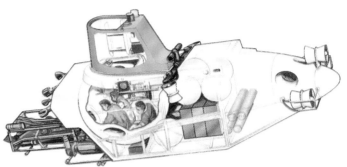

Smokers were first photographed by the submersible *Alvin*, a miniature submarine that can carry only 3 people. It has all sorts of equipment on the outside, such as cameras and lights, which can be operated by the people inside.

Some areas around warm-water vents are inhabited by many big snails, rather than by clams and tube worms. These are called "hairy" snails because their shells are covered by little spines that look like hair. Like other smoker animals, they probably feed on bacteria and sulfur.

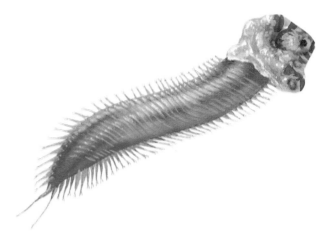

Pompeii worms live near some warm-water vents. They are named after the Roman town that was destroyed when a volcano erupted. Living near a smoker is like living near a volcano.

What is a tsunami?

Tsunamis, or tidal waves, are the biggest waves of all. Unlike other waves on the sea surface, tsunamis are not formed by winds and storms and have nothing to do with the tides. They happen when an earthquake or volcanic eruption occurs under the sea, pushing a huge mass of water through the ocean at speeds of up to 500 miles per hour. In the past many people died because tsunamis struck without warning. One tsunami hit the island of Honshu in Japan in 1896, drowning 26,000 people and destroying over 100,000 homes. Today earthquakes and eruptions throughout the world are monitored in Hawaii, and people are warned if a wave is expected so that they can move inland to safety.

More about tsunamis

Out in the deep ocean, a tsunami might not be obvious. Although it moves very quickly, it is stretched out over long distances and may be only 3 feet high. But as it reaches shallow water closer to shore, it slows down. Its height increases rapidly to about 150 feet before it crashes down with tremendous force on the shore.

The highest recorded tsunami happened off Ishigaki Island, Japan, in 1971. The height of the wave was estimated to be 280 feet, which is nearly as high as the Statue of Liberty.

The damage caused by a tsunami can be devastating. Thousands of homes may be demolished, trees uprooted, and boats and cars washed away. Hundreds, even thousands, of people may lose their lives.

How do we get oil from the ocean floor?

Oil from the ocean floor is extracted by oil rigs. A drill bores down into the ocean floor and pumps up the oil. The oil is taken to land in underwater pipes or by tankers. Several hundred people live on the platform of an oil rig, and each person stays there for about two weeks at a time. They include engineers, mechanics who look after the machinery, deep-sea divers who check the pipes, and many others. They are taken to the rig by ship or by helicopter.

More about oil

Oil collects in the tiny holes of porous rocks, such as sandstone and limestone, like water in a sponge. Some oil lies as much as 1 or 2 miles under the ocean floor. Modern equipment helps the oil companies to locate the likely spots where oil might be found.

About 3 million tons of oil from ships, refineries, and harbors spill into the sea each year. This often kills or poisons wildlife. Seabirds can die, because the oil clogs up their feathers so that they cannot fly. When they try to clean themselves, they eat the oil, which poisons them.

What happens when ships sink?

The sea is a very dangerous place in bad weather, and ships sometimes sink. Many cargo ships sank in the Mediterranean Sea as long ago as Greek and Roman times. The food, pots, and other goods that the ships were carrying can still be found in the sunken wrecks. Many battleships have been sunk during wars. In World War II, hundreds of ships were lost in the Pacific. Some, like this Japanese destroyer, have become beautiful "artificial" reefs. It is covered with seaweed, corals, and other animals and provides a home for hundreds of fish.

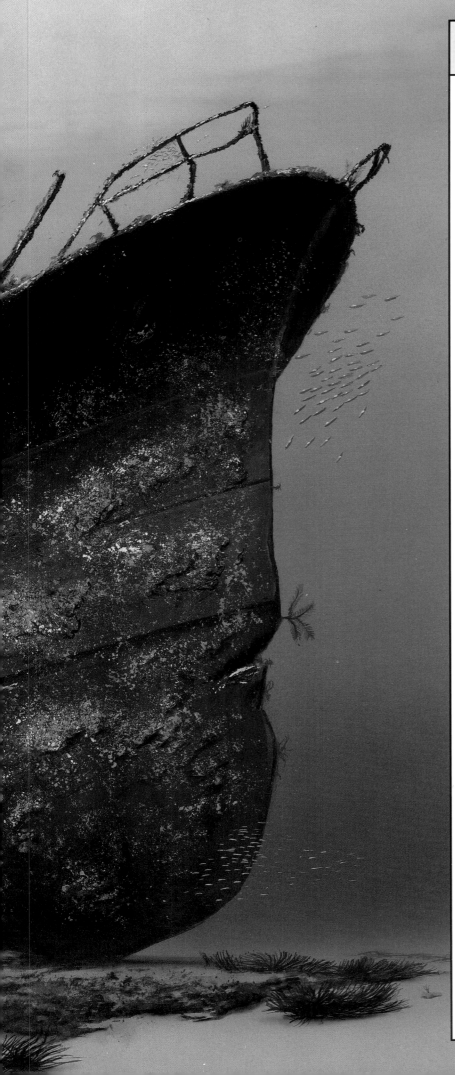

More about shipwrecks

The *Titanic* was a British passenger liner that sank in 1912 on her first voyage across the Atlantic Ocean. The ship collided with an iceberg at night and sank in just over two hours. More than 1,500 people drowned, but about 700 were saved by other ships that came to the rescue.

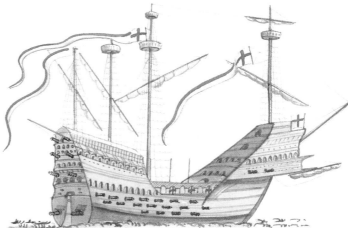

The *Mary Rose* was the warship of King Henry VIII of England. She sank off the southern coast of England in 1545 with the loss of more than 600 lives. The wreck was not discovered until 1970 and was raised in 1982. It is now on public display.

Long ago, ships often carried gold and silver, jewelry, money, and other treasure. Many of these ships were wrecked in storms, and their treasure sank with them. Today people search for shipwrecks to find the sunken treasure.

More about underwater exploration

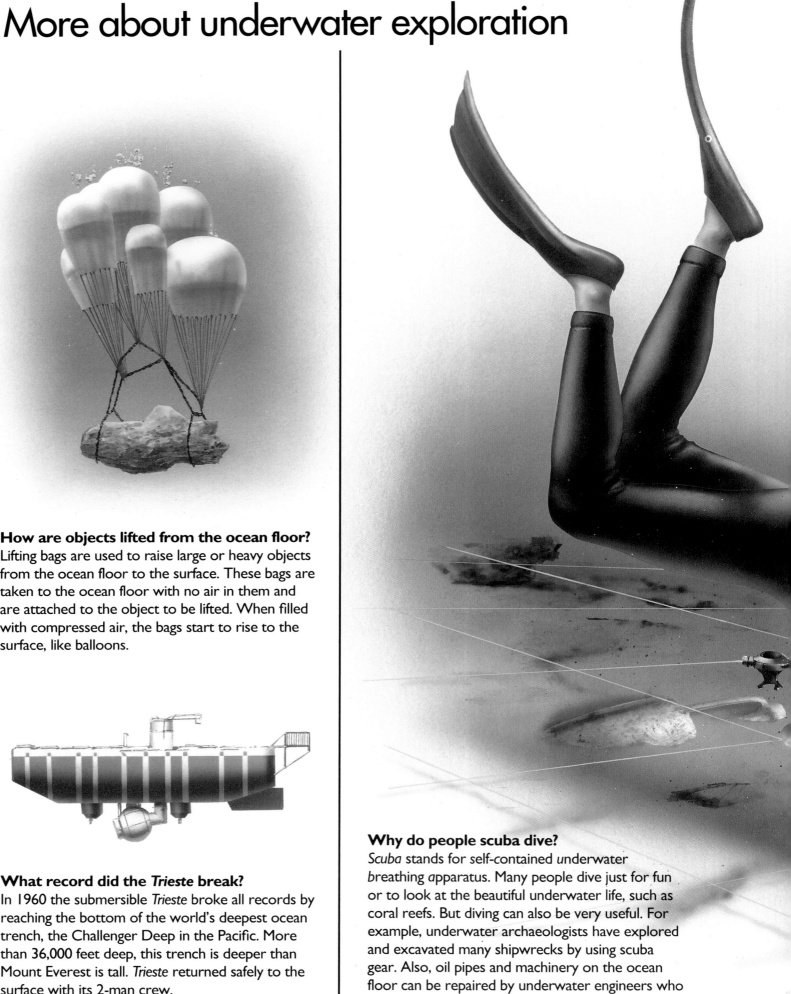

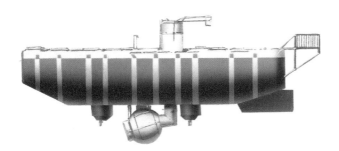

How are objects lifted from the ocean floor?
Lifting bags are used to raise large or heavy objects from the ocean floor to the surface. These bags are taken to the ocean floor with no air in them and are attached to the object to be lifted. When filled with compressed air, the bags start to rise to the surface, like balloons.

What record did the *Trieste* break?
In 1960 the submersible *Trieste* broke all records by reaching the bottom of the world's deepest ocean trench, the Challenger Deep in the Pacific. More than 36,000 feet deep, this trench is deeper than Mount Everest is tall. *Trieste* returned safely to the surface with its 2-man crew.

Why do people scuba dive?
Scuba stands for self-contained underwater breathing apparatus. Many people dive just for fun or to look at the beautiful underwater life, such as coral reefs. But diving can also be very useful. For example, underwater archaeologists have explored and excavated many shipwrecks by using scuba gear. Also, oil pipes and machinery on the ocean floor can be repaired by underwater engineers who use scuba equipment.

How are photographs taken underwater?
Underwater photography is a very popular hobby with scuba divers and is useful for archaeologists and scientists. The cameras they use must be waterproof and have a strong, pressure-proof casing. A good flashbulb is essential to show up all the colors. Remote-controlled cameras can take photos in the deepest parts of the ocean. These photographs show us things that would not normally be seen by humans.

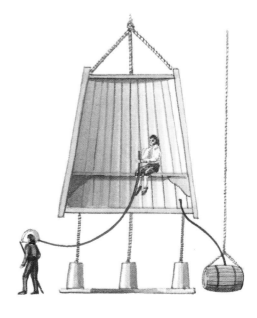

How did people dive long ago?
The first successful underwater "dives" were carried out in the early seventeenth century in diving bells. These were lowered to the bottom of the sea with lead weights. Air was trapped inside the bell, and the diver could walk away from the bell, breathing the air through a hose connected to the bell.

Why do we use submersibles?
The modern Johnson *Sea-Link* submersible, which carries 2 people, can dive to 1,500 feet. The occupants can put on scuba gear and climb out the back into the water. Various gadgets are attached to the outside of the submersible, such as cameras and lights. Submersibles like this are used for laying pipelines, repairing oil rigs, finding wrecks, and for scientific work.

Where do turtles lay their eggs?

Female marine turtles travel hundreds of miles to lay their eggs, often returning to the beaches where they were born. On some beaches in India and Mexico, thousands of turtles gather at the same time every year. They usually come ashore at night, when there are fewer predators around, hauling themselves slowly up across the sand. When they have found a suitable spot, they dig a hole, scraping the sand away with their hind flippers. They lay their eggs in the hole. The turtles cover the eggs — sometimes more than 100 at a time — with sand and go back to the sea before morning comes.

More about turtles

When baby loggerhead turtles hatch, they are only a few inches long. They scramble up through the sand onto the beach and run straight down into the sea. Unfortunately, many are eaten by seabirds and other animals before they get to the water.

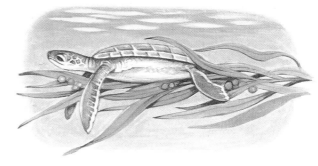

Young turtles are probably carried on big rafts of seaweed by ocean currents. They may get carried all the way across the Atlantic like this, finding food in the seaweed and sometimes ending up in Europe!

The huge leatherback is the largest marine turtle. It may weigh up to half a ton and be nearly 7 feet long. Unlike other turtles, which have shells, this turtle has bony platelets covered with a leathery skin, which gives it its name. Leatherback turtles have become very rare now, and concerned people are trying to save them.

Why does a walrus change color?

Like all marine mammals, the walrus has a thick layer of fat, called blubber, under its skin to keep it warm. But this can also make it difficult to keep cool. When a walrus is underwater, it is pale gray in color. But when it comes out of the water into warmer air, particularly on sunny days, it turns a pinkish-beige color. This is because the blood comes to the surface of the skin so that the walrus can cool off. The tusks of a walrus are huge teeth. Walruses use their tusks to pull themselves out of the water onto ice floes. They also fight with their tusks, and the largest walrus with the largest tusks usually wins.

M CAMM

Which whales sing songs?

Humpback whales are famous for singing songs underwater. They sing a wide variety of songs that can be heard hundreds of miles away. No one knows exactly why these whales sing. Humpbacks are also among the most acrobatic of whales. Like some other whales, they can leap, or "breach," right out of the water. Humpback whales can even do backward somersaults! Whales breathe through blowholes on the tops of their heads. The spout of water, which is formed when the whale exhales, can be seen from far away.

CAMM

More about whales

Sometimes whales come close to the shore and become stranded on beaches. Pilot whales, which look like large dolphins, live in large groups called schools and often become stranded. No one is quite sure why this happens, but it may be because the whales get lost or confused.

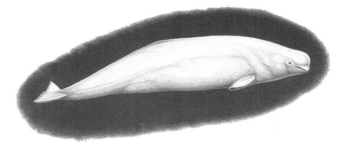

The beluga whale is unusual because it is white and often looks as if it is smiling. It makes a variety of noises and is sometimes called the "canary of the sea." It lives in large groups, or herds, sometimes numbering hundreds or thousands.

Whales have been hunted for hundreds of years for their meat and oil. Big factory whaling ships, which first appeared in the 1920s, were used to catch and kill hundreds of them. Many whales are now very rare, but conservation organizations are trying to protect them.

Which animals live on coral reefs?

Coral reefs grow in warm, shallow waters. They are built by coral colonies and all the other plants and animals that live in and on the reef. They are home to an enormous variety of colorful plants, fish, and other animals. Angelfish and butterfly fish are especially brightly colored. Small sharks cruise along the edge of a reef, looking for other fish to eat. Fish, such as moray eels, live in holes in the reef — half-hidden and ready to pounce on small fish as they pass by. Some coral reef fish eat seaweed.

More about corals

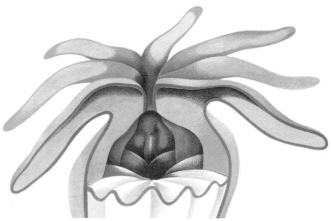

The coral animal itself is a tiny creature called a polyp. It is like a little sea anemone. The polyp makes a stony, cup-shaped skeleton to support itself and divides to form new polyps. A group of polyps like this is called a coral colony.

The crown-of-thorns starfish is one of the few animals that eat corals. It sucks the living parts out, leaving a white skeleton behind. Sometimes huge numbers of these starfish appear on reefs, such as the Great Barrier Reef in Australia, and kill large areas of coral.

Corals, like many marine animals, reproduce by releasing their eggs and sperm in the water. This is called spawning. The sperm fertilizes the egg, and a tiny new coral starts to grow.

More about small ocean creatures

What is an anemone?
Once called "flower animals," sea anemones are among the prettiest animals in the sea. They are like upside-down jellyfish. Anemones live attached to rocks or buried in the mud, waving their tentacles to catch food. Some are tiny, less than an inch high, but others are enormous. In the tropics, some may grow to 3 feet in diameter.

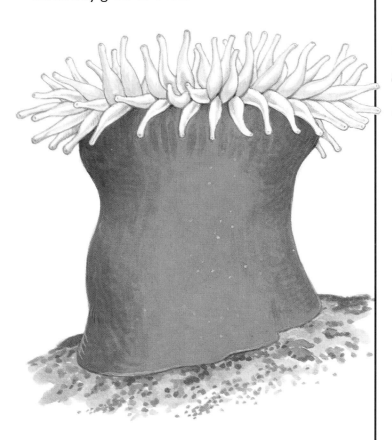

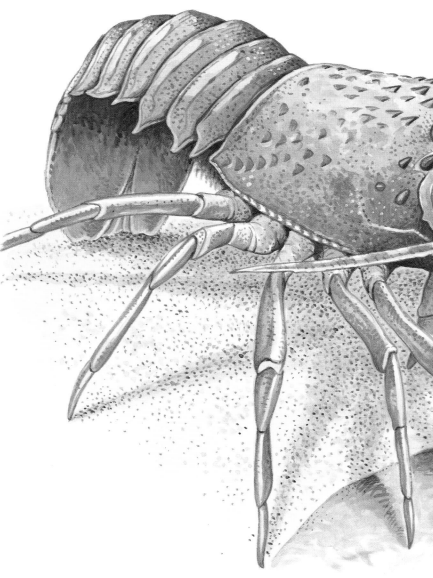

Where do hermit crabs live?
Unlike most crabs, hermit crabs have soft bodies. They have to live inside the shells of mollusks to protect themselves. As they grow, they leave these shells and find bigger ones.

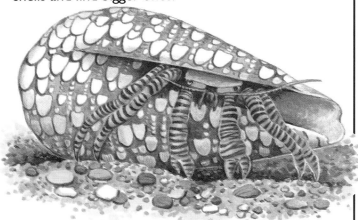

Why are sea slugs brightly colored?
Sea slugs, or nudibranchs, have no shell. They are poisonous, which protects them from being eaten by other animals. To warn animals that they are poisonous, sea slugs are often beautifully colored and patterned. The tentacles on their backs are really gills, which are used for breathing. Many sea slugs feed on corals and sponges.

Which animal has a suit of armor?

Lobsters and crabs are like knights in armor with their hard, jointed outer skeleton to protect them. When this armor, or cuticle, gets too small, it splits. The lobster climbs out backward. A new cuticle develops, which is big enough for the lobster to grow inside.

How do scallops move?

When scallops snap their two shells together, a current of water shoots out and makes them hop along the ocean floor. Scallops have brightly colored eyes around the edges of their shells.

Why are sea urchins prickly?

Many small ocean creatures are prickly or poisonous to stop fish and other animals from eating them. Sea urchins are some of the spiniest animals in the sea. You should be careful not to step on them.

Which worm is furry?

One of the strangest-looking worms in the world is the sea mouse. It does not look like a worm at all, because it is covered with fine, silky bristles that look like fur. It lives in shallow water, just below the surface of the sand or mud.

What is a goose barnacle?

Egg-shaped goose barnacles are, surprisingly, related to shrimps and crabs. They stick their legs out of their shells and wave them around to catch food. They live attached to rocks by their stalks and are frequently found on driftwood, bottles, and other floating debris.

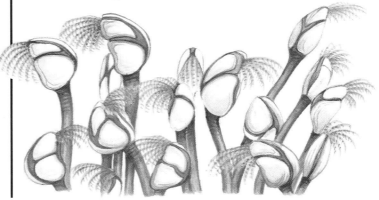

Where are icebergs found?

Snows that fall on the island of Greenland and the continent of Antarctica form deep ice fields called glaciers. These glaciers flow from the land into the sea, where each year huge chunks break off to form icebergs. An iceberg can be 200 feet high, like a huge cliff. But this is only a small part of the whole iceberg — since 90 percent of it is underwater!

Large colonies of albatrosses, penguins, other seabirds, and seals are found on Antarctic shores. Penguins look funny waddling around on land, but underwater they are very fast and agile. They hunt for fish, using their flipperlike wings as paddles.

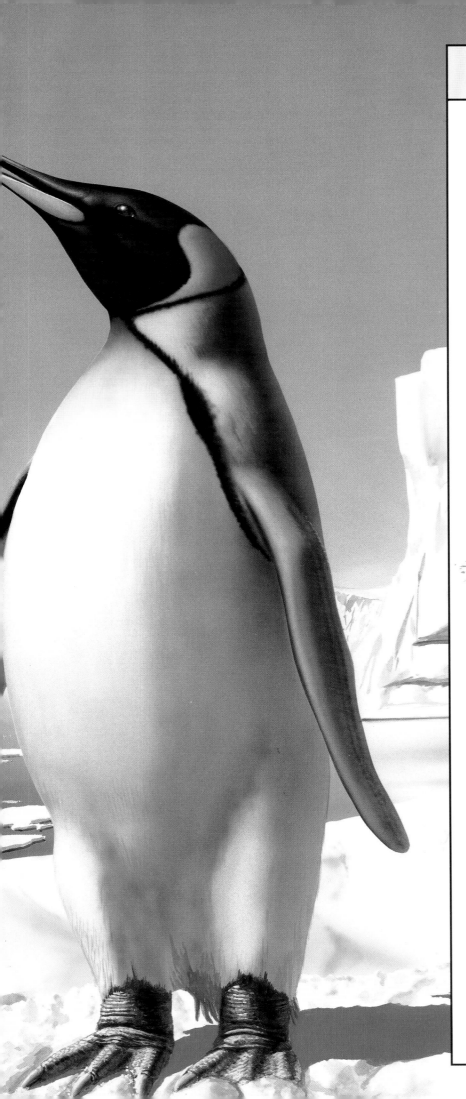

More about the Antarctic

Weddell seals live in the Antarctic. They can dive deeper than any other seal and can stay underwater for more than an hour. If they come up under the ice, they can make breathing holes with their teeth.

Pack ice, which forms when the sea freezes, is a big problem for ships. Icebreakers have specially strengthened hulls that can break through the ice. Other ships can then travel through the channel that the icebreakers make.

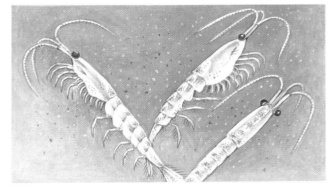

Krill live in huge groups, or "swarms," in the Antarctic Ocean. They look like shrimp, and are eaten in enormous quantities by fish, penguins, and whales. A single whale can consume 4 or 5 tons of krill in a day.

What do mangrove trees look like?

Mangrove trees grow on muddy coasts in warm regions. Their roots are able to survive the salty water. Since there is little oxygen in the mud, some of the roots grow in the air to help the mangroves breathe. Sometimes these roots grow down from branches, or they stick up like little chimneys from the mud. All kinds of animals live here, including crocodiles, crabs, and fish. Many birds, such as egrets and red ibis, roost in the mangrove trees, feeding on fish and smaller animals in the water and mud below.

More about mangrove animals

One of the biggest animals that lives in mangrove swamps is the saltwater crocodile. It can grow to 25 feet long. It lays its eggs in a large mound of rotting plants, which keeps the eggs warm.

Mudskippers are little fish that can walk over the mud by using their front fins. They can also move in little skips by flicking their tails. They breathe through gills, but unlike other fish they carry a supply of water in their gills to help them breathe when they are on land.

Mangroves are full of crabs, such as soldier crabs and fiddler crabs, which scuttle over the mud between the roots at low tide. The male fiddler crab has an enormous claw that is used to warn off rivals and to attract females.

Where did Columbus sail to?

The Italian explorer Christopher Columbus first set sail from Palos, Spain, in 1492. He sailed across the Atlantic Ocean with 90 men. They sailed in three ships — the flagship *Santa María* and the smaller *Niña* and *Pinta*. He wanted to find a quick route to India, but instead he landed in the Bahamas. Columbus made four voyages to the New World and discovered many other Caribbean islands and the coasts of Central and South America. But all the time, he thought he was in India — and that is why the Caribbean islands are still often referred to as the West Indies.

More about great ocean voyages

Where did *Ra II* sail?

In 1970 the explorer Thor Heyerdahl sailed across the Atlantic, from Morocco in Africa to Barbados in the West Indies, in a boat made of bundles of papyrus reeds. He did this to prove that a journey across the Atlantic Ocean could have been made by ancient peoples, such as the Egyptians.

Where did Captain Cook explore?

The Englishman Captain James Cook was one of the greatest ocean explorers. He sailed around the world three times between 1768 and 1779. He explored Australia and many of the Pacific islands. He was killed in Hawaii in 1779 as a result of a misunderstanding between his crew and the local people over a stolen boat.

Sextant   **Astrolabe**

What is a clipper?

In the nineteenth century clipper ships carried goods from Europe and America to Asia, Australia, and New Zealand, returning with wool, tea, and other goods. They crossed the oceans at great speed, making use of the trade winds. The fastest voyage by a clipper from Australia to England took 59 days.

Where did the Vikings explore?

Most people think that Christopher Columbus was the first European to visit America. However, Columbus was not the first to cross the Atlantic Ocean. The Vikings crossed the Atlantic many years before him. In their long, wooden boats, powered by as many as 60 rowers, the Vikings discovered Iceland and Greenland. From there, they went on to find Newfoundland.

How did early sailors navigate?

Early sailors had to use the stars, the sun, and the moon to find their way across the oceans. Special instruments were invented to help with this. The astrolabe was used to map the stars. The sextant measured the angle of the sun and stars above the horizon. We now have radar and other modern methods to help with navigation.

Who first explored the Pacific Ocean?

The Polynesians were the very first explorers of the Pacific Ocean. They traveled great distances in their double canoes in search of new islands. They used the stars and the sun to guide them. They could also tell if land was near by the shape and color of clouds, by smells in the wind, and by the presence of seabirds.

Where are a hammerhead shark's eyes?

The hammerhead shark is one of the strangest-looking sharks. Its eyes are on the ends of big knobs on either side of its head. This may help it to find other fish to eat. Although hammerhead sharks have occasionally attacked humans, most other kinds of sharks do not hurt people. Most feed on fish, and some live on the ocean floor and have flat teeth for crushing shells and eating the animals inside. Sharks have very rough skin that is covered with little toothlike bumps, called denticles. Unlike many other fish whose skeleton is made of bone, the skeleton of a shark is made of "cartilage."

More about sharks

Nurse sharks spend most of their time on the ocean floor and are very sluggish compared to other kinds of sharks. Often, if they are disturbed, they will crawl away on their fins instead of swimming.

The great white shark occasionally attacks humans, but this is rare. It usually eats seals and porpoises. Sometimes a human on a surfboard may look like a seal to a shark swimming underwater.

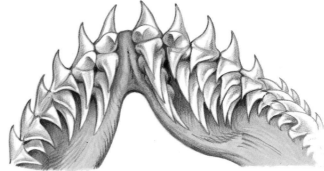

Some sharks have up to 3,000 teeth in their mouth, arranged in as many as 20 rows. Only the first couple of rows are used for feeding. The rest move forward to replace the front ones as they wear out.

How big is the giant octopus?

The giant Pacific octopus, or "devilfish," can grow up to 10 feet in diameter. It swims either by "parachuting," when it stretches all its tentacles out and floats up and down, or by "jetting," when it squirts out a jet of water behind it and shoots forward. Though it usually feeds on crabs, devilfish have been known to shoot out of the water and grab seabirds. Like other octopuses, it can change its color from bright red to white. It can also make its skin spiky or smooth. The octopus is a "mollusk." Although it looks very different, it is related to animals with shells, such as snails and clams.

More about mollusks

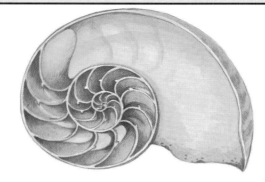

The chambered nautilus floats in the ocean. It feeds near the surface at night, using its tentacles to catch food, and then sinks to the safety of deep water during the daytime. Inside its shell are "chambers" of air that help it to float.

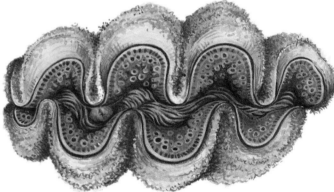

The giant clam has one of the biggest shells in the world and can weigh over 200 pounds. Its "mantle," the section that shows between the two parts of the shell, is often brilliant blue or green. The world's giant clam population has been depleted by people who collect the shells and who eat the tasty meat.

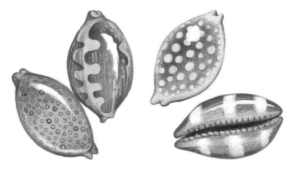

Cowries have beautiful, shiny, patterned shells. People have collected them for hundreds of years, and in some countries they were once used as money. Underwater, the mantle comes out of the shell and covers it up completely when the animal is feeding and moving.

How does a jellyfish sting?

Jellyfish are aptly named. They are like big blobs of floating jelly, and even the firmest are made mostly of water. They swim by opening and closing their umbrella-shaped bodies, which are often beautifully colored. Some, like this one called *Pelagia noctiluca*, become luminous at night.

Many jellyfish can inflict a painful sting with their tentacles, which are also used for catching food. The Portuguese man-of-war is one of the most dangerous animals in the sea, but it is not a true jellyfish. It is a colony of animals of the same species that floats on the surface of the water.

More about weird creatures of the deep

How did the sea pen get its name?

The central spine of a sea pen looks like the quill of a feather. This creature was given its name in the days when people used quills as pens. It lives on the bottom of the sea with its stalk buried in mud. Some sea pens also produce waves of phosphorescence, or glowing light, if disturbed.

How big is a giant squid?

Giant squid, which grow up to 70 feet long, may be responsible for stories about monsters from the deep. However, it seems unlikely that a giant squid would wrap its tentacles around a ship and sink it. Squid can swim very fast, and some of the small squid that live near the surface of the water even shoot out and fly through the air.

What is a glass sponge?

Glass sponges look nothing like the sponges we use in the kitchen or bathroom. Their skeletons are made of glasslike silica, which form a delicate lattice. One of the most beautiful is the Venus flower basket. Like all sponges, they feed by filtering tiny plants and animals out of the water that flows through their bodies.

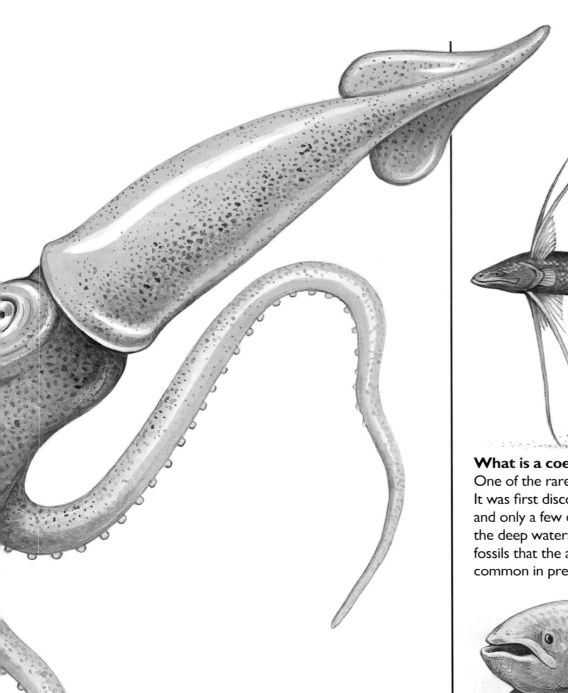

What is a tripod fish?

Much of the bottom of the deep sea is covered with a thick layer of soft mud and sand. To keep them from sinking in, tripod fish have stiffened fins and tails on which they rest.

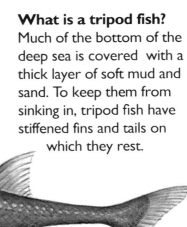

What is a coelacanth?

One of the rarest fish in the world is the coelacanth. It was first discovered in 1938 in the Indian Ocean, and only a few dozen have ever been caught from the deep waters in which it lives. We know from fossils that the ancestors of coelacanths were common in prehistoric times.

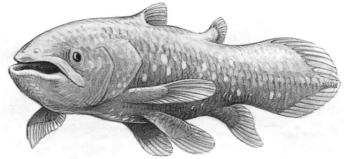

Which fish have lights?

Many deep-sea fish produce light to attract food and help them see in the dark depths of the oceans. Lantern fish are speckled with lights, which look like little dots. They also have large glands near their tails that produce light. Lantern fish are very sensitive to light signals.

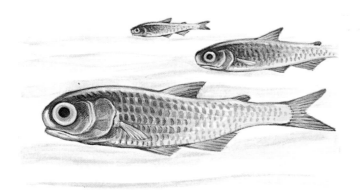

Which fish has an elastic stomach?

One of the ugliest fish in the ocean must be the angler fish with its lumpy body and huge mouth. It uses the luminous lure above its mouth to attract food. Angler fish have elastic stomachs that can stretch to fit huge amounts of food — an angler fish was found with an eel, 3 fish, and 5 shrimp in its stomach.

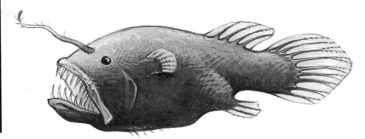

Where do seabirds gather to breed?

Many seabirds gather in big groups, or colonies, to mate on cliffs or rocky islets during the breeding season. The males and females pair off. Often the same couples mate every year throughout their lives. Puffins have brightly colored beaks to help them attract mates. Each pair of puffins uses their beaks to dig a burrow on a grassy cliff. At the end of the burrow, the female lays a single egg, which later hatches into a chick.

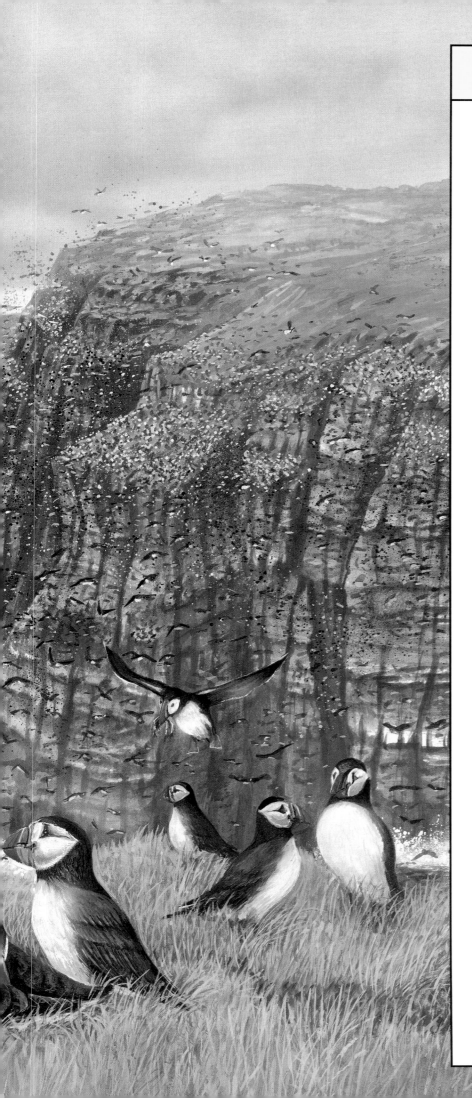

More about seabirds

When the brown pelican spots a school of fish, it will plunge down into the sea vertically. Then it will swim along with its huge beak and pouch open, scooping up its meal.

Albatrosses can glide over the sea for hours on their enormous wings. The wings of the wandering albatross stretch 12 feet from tip to tip. As it skims over the surface, the albatross feeds by grabbing fish or squid from the water.

The fairy, or white, tern lives in the tropics, but unlike many seabirds does not live in colonies. It lays a single egg — often balanced on the branch of a tree.

How are fish caught?

Modern fishing boats use huge nets to catch large numbers of fish. Purse seine nets are used for catching whole schools at once. The net, which may be hundreds of feet long, is set up in a big circle around the fish. The ropes at the top and bottom of the net are then pulled in tight, like a drawstring purse, and the fish are caught inside. Fish are an important source of food in many countries.

However, overfishing in many parts of the world means that too many fish have been taken from the sea. If this keeps happening, the supply of fish may run out.

More about fishing

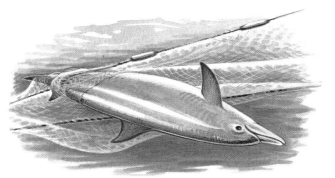

The huge drift nets used to catch tuna, salmon, and squid also accidentally catch other animals, such as dolphins. Thousands of dolphins drown in these nets because they cannot get to the surface to breathe. These nets are now banned in the United States and many other countries.

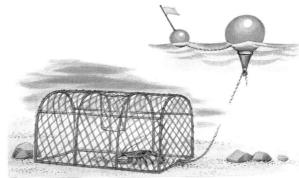

Animals on the ocean floor can be caught in pots or traps that are often baited with scraps of fish or other food. A lobster can get into a lobster pot easily through the hole in the top. However, once in the pot, it is almost impossible for the lobster to get out again.

Fishermen around the world have found many different ways to catch fish. In some places in Sri Lanka, they sit high up on stilts over the water. The fishermen can easily see the fish below, but the fish cannot see them. The fish are caught with spears.

Index

AN ILEX BOOK
Created and produced by Ilex Publishers Limited
29-31 George Street, Oxford, OX1 2AY

Main illustrations by Sebastian Quigley/Linden Artists
Other illustrations by David Thelwell/Bernard Thornton Artists
David Wright, Mike Saunders/Kathy Jakeman Illustration Martin Camm